Our Funny Feelings

at

Monstrocity School

By Anjali Sawhney

This book is dedicated to all of the people who have supported me to get to where I am today.

COCKADOODLEDOO!!
"Ari, it's time to wake up!" called Mummy softly.

Ari woke up with a big smile on her face. She was excited for her first day of school. Going to school may seem scary to some children, but not to Ari. She could not wait to embark on her new adventure at Monstrocity School.

When they arrived at school,
Ari looked around her and saw huuuugge
buildings and giants which towered over her.

As Mummy took Ari to the entrance, she was
greeted by Miss Morgan,
"Hello Ari! I know, it looks very scary but we will
have a really fun day."
"I don't feel well, Mummy." murmured Ari.
"You'll be fine. You were so excited before!"
Mummy replied.

"Oh dear, do we have a funny feeling?" asked
Miss Morgan.
Ari nodded.

Miss Morgan took Ari's arms and spoke to her softly,
"When we have a funny feeling,
We can see what it's revealing.
Do we have a funny feeling, Ari?"
Ari nodded.

"We've got a funny feeling,
Where oh where is it appearing?
Where is the funny feeling in your body?"
Ari pointed to her tummy.

She felt like there was a swarm of butterflies fluttering around inside her tummy.

"They are friendly, fluttering butterflies and they are ready to come out of your tummy.
Can you help to set them free?" asked Miss Morgan.
Ari nodded.

"Close your eyes and picture the friendly, fluttering butterflies in your tummy. Take a big breath in and blow all of those butterflies away."

With each breath, Ari felt more butterflies leaving her tummy.
"Are you feeling better now?" asked Miss Morgan.

Just like that, Ari didn't feel the friendly, fluttering butterflies in her tummy and she was ready for a fun day at school.

After a morning of lessons, it was playtime. Ari looked around the playground to see who she could play with but no one wanted to play with her.

Ari looked down. She started to feel a funny feeling as she stood alone.
What was she to do?!
Miss Morgan saw Ari walking alone and went over to speak to her,
"Ari, are you okay?"
Ari looked down with a droopy face.
"Shall we find you someone to play with?"
Ari shrugged her shoulders.

"Do you remember our rhyme?" asked Miss Morgan.

Ari nodded so Miss Morgan continued,
"When we have a funny feeling,
We can see what it's revealing.
Do we have a funny feeling?"
Ari nodded.

"We've got a funny feeling,
Where oh where is it appearing?
Where is the funny feeling in your body?"
Ari pointed to her heart.

"Does it feel like your heart is melting into your tummy?" asked Miss Morgan.
She nodded.

"Picture a flickering candle that is melting your heart into your tummy. That is a friendly, flickering candle that wants to be blown out. Can you help to blow out the candle?"
Ari nodded.

"Take a big breath in and blow out the candle."
After a few big breaths, Ari looked up at Miss
Morgan with a smile. Miss Morgan took her hand
and led her to play with a group of children.

But soon after, Ari's new friends didn't want to play with her anymore. They walked away and she stood alone again. What was she to do?

The bell rang and Ari went back into class
feeling rather sad and blue.
She did NOT want to feel those funny
feelings again.

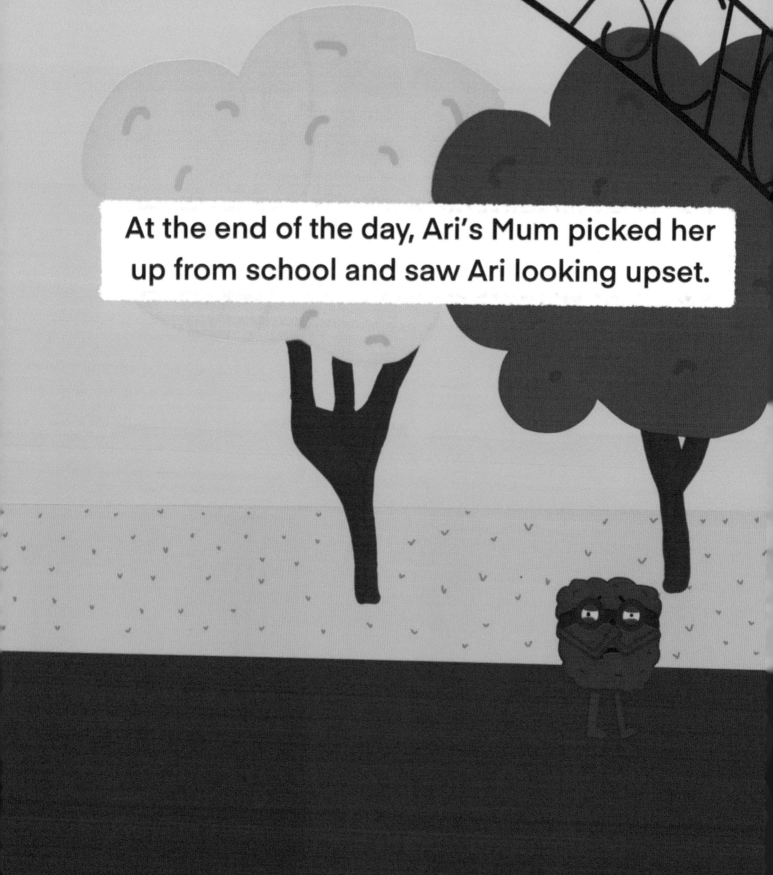

At the end of the day, Ari's Mum picked her up from school and saw Ari looking upset.

"Whatever is the matter, Ari?" asked Mummy.
"I don't want to go to school. No one wants to
play with me," cried Ari.

"It will be ok, Ari. They are all still getting used
to being at school. You will make friends soon.
Be brave and use your big, loud voice." said
Mummy positively.

The next day, Ari went back to school. She remembered what Mummy said about her big, loud voice and she went into school ready for the first lesson of the day. Scaring practice.

Ari looked across the classroom to see the other children with smiles after letting out loud roars to scare people.
But each time she tried, her roar was not loud enough! No one took notice of her and her roar.
What was she to do?!

"I can't do it!" shouted Ari.
She stomped her feet and clenched her fists with a
frown on her face.

Miss Morgan saw Ari's face turning red and went over
to help her.
"Ari, do you remember our rhyme?" asked Miss
Morgan.

They both said it together.

"When we have a funny feeling,
We can see what it's revealing.
Do we have a funny feeling, Ari?"
She nodded.

"We've got a funny feeling,
Where oh where is it appearing?
Where is the funny feeling in your body?"
She pointed to her face.

"Do we have a hot dragon head?" asked Miss Morgan.
Ari nodded.

"Close your eyes and picture that hot fire coming out of your dragon head. That is a friendly dragon and it wants to blow out all of its angry fire and we can help our friendly dragon to blow it out," said Miss Morgan with a soft and quiet voice.

After a few big breaths, Ari looked up at Miss Morgan with a big smile ready to try scaring practice again.
Her funny feelings were gone and she carried on having fun for the rest of the day.

The next day, Ari woke up with a grin on her face.
When she got to school, she looked around and saw another monster with a worried face.

Ari went over to them and said,
"Hello, when we have a funny feeling,
We can see what it's revealing.
Do you have a funny feeling?"
Zac, the other monster, nodded.

"We've got a funny feeling,
Where oh where is it appearing?
Where is the funny feeling in your body, Zac?"
continued Ari.
Zac pointed to his tummy.

"You have butterflies too! Close your eyes and picture the butterflies in your tummy. They are friendly, fluttering butterflies and they want to be blown out. Take a big breath in and blow them all out."

Just like that, Zac looked at Ari with a smile.
They walked to the entrance together where they saw Miss
Morgan and Ari couldn't wait to tell her how she helped Zac.
"Miss Morgan, I helped my friend with his funny feelings!"
shouted Ari excitedly.
"Wow Ari! Well done for helping Zac! You are such a good
friend. I am so, so, SO proud of you," replied Miss Morgan.

Now Ari would always know how to help herself AND others
when they felt a funny feeling.

Printed in Great Britain
by Amazon